W9-AVL-974

Princess Penelopea Hates Peas

A Tale of Picky Eating and Avoiding Catastropeas

by Susan D. Sweet, PhD
and Brenda S. Miles, PhD

illustrated by
Valeria Docampo

MAGINATION PRESS · WASHINGTON, DC
American Psychological Association

For my family, believers in dreams—SDS

For Katherine and Brian, child advocates who venture forth with passion and creativity—BSM

With love for the little princess Helena—VD

Published by
MAGINATION PRESS ®
An Educational Publishing Foundation Book
American Psychological Association
750 First Street NE
Washington, DC 20002

Magination Press is a registered trademark of the American Psychological Association.

For more information about our books, including a complete catalog, please write to us, call 1-800-374-2721, or visit our website at www.apa.org/pubs/magination.

Book design by Susan K. White
Printed by Phoenix Color Corporation, Hagerstown, MD

Library of Congress Cataloging-in-Publication Data
Sweet, Susan D.
Princess Penelopea hates peas : a tale of picky eating
and avoiding catastropeas / by Susan D. Sweet, PhD
and Brenda S. Miles, PhD.
pages cm
"American Psychological Association."
Summary: "Penolopea lives in Capital Pea where peas are plentiful and popular.
The problem is that Penolopea hates peas! So she comes up with a plan to make them
disappear only leading to a catastropea of epic portions. Eventually, Penolopea grows
her own plant and tastes one perfect pea. Turns out, she likes peas after all!"—
Provided by publisher.
ISBN 978-1-4338-2046-5 (hardcover) — ISBN 1-4338-2046-3 (hardcover)
[1. Princesses—Fiction. 2. Food habits—Fiction. 3. Peas—Fiction.] I. Miles, Brenda. II. Title.
PZ7.1.S93Pr 2016
[E]—dc23   2015014436

Manufactured in the United States of America
First printing October 2015
10 9 8 7 6 5 4 3 2 1

Once upon a time there lived a princess named Penelopea.
Penelopea hated peas. She wouldn't touch them or smell them,
and she certainly wouldn't eat them!

She even hated the p~e~a in her name,
so she wrote her name without it.

But hating peas was a problem because Penelopea lived in Capital Pea, a kingdom where peas were very popular. People grew them, sold them, and ate them by the pound—poached, pureed, and pan-fried!

The king and queen tried to change her mind. "You should eat your peas," they would say. "Peas are **pea**-licious!"

That didn't work, so they tried hiding peas in Penelopea's porridge. But she found every single one and then she stopped eating porridge.

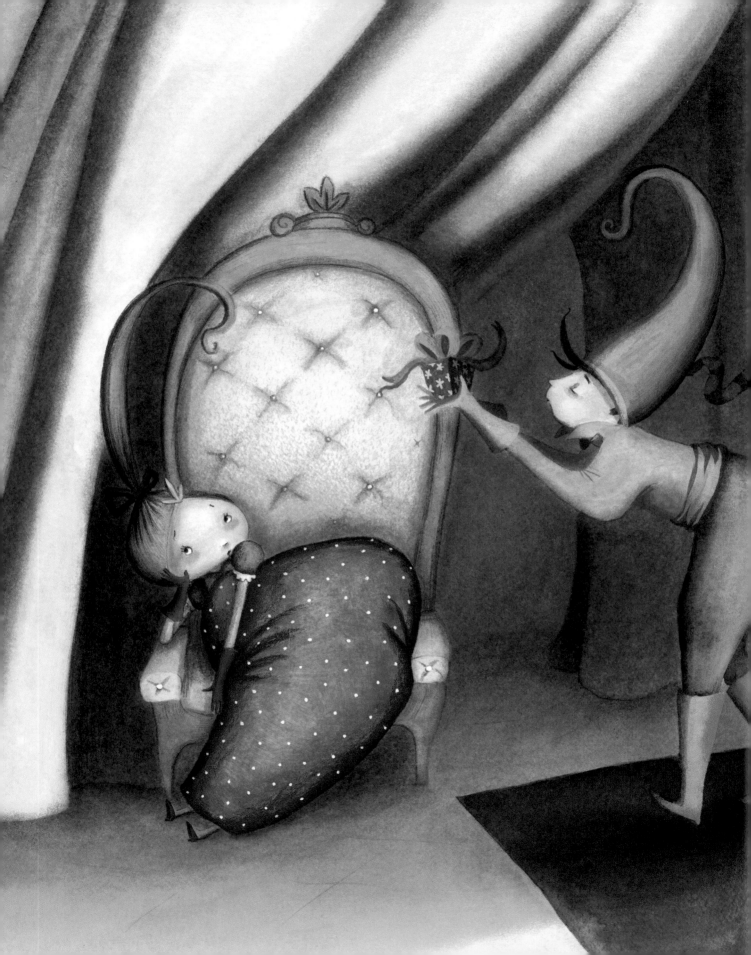

Next her parents
promised presents if she
ate her peas, but the
princess only pouted.

Finally the king and queen grew angry.
"You will make those peas disappear!" they said.

Then Penelopea had an idea.

And the peas did disappear...

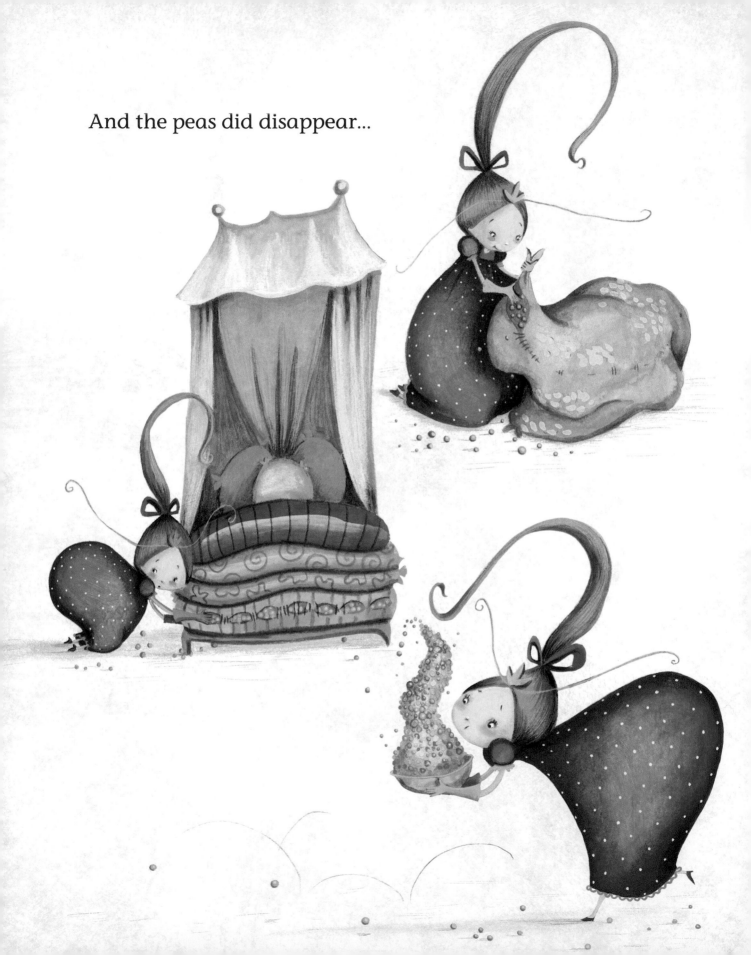

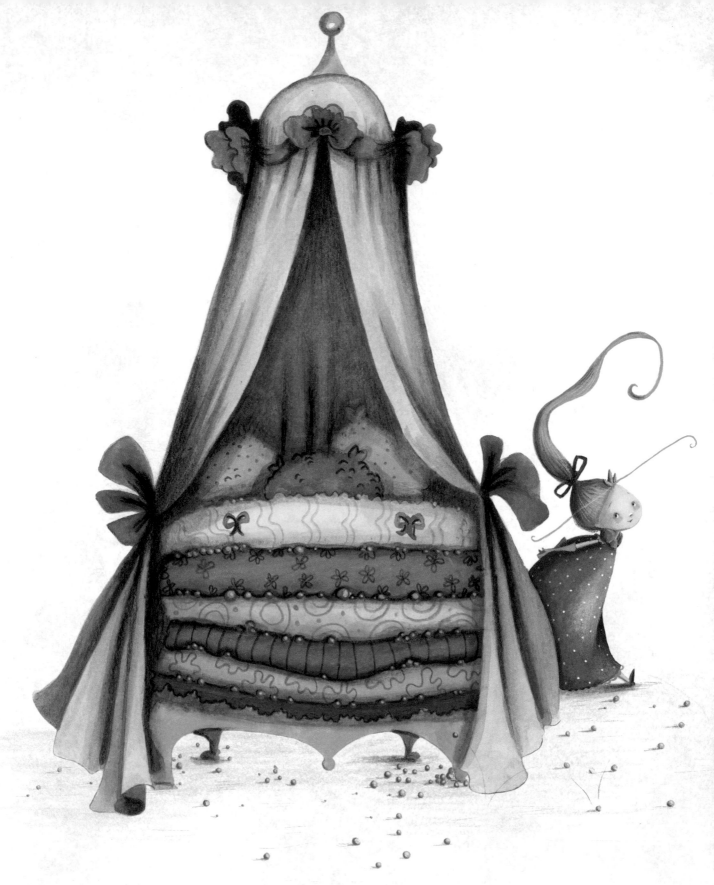

one mattress at a time.

Penelopea's plan seemed to work.
The king and queen were pleased
because they thought she had
eaten her peas.

But, really, those peas were packed in mattresses all over the kingdom.

Then, one night, when everyone jumped into bed...

Squish! Splat! Catastropea!

Green goo was everywhere! The king and queen
were not pleased. "No more peas!" they said,
and they ordered all peas out of the kingdom.

"Perfect!" said Penelopea...until she found one last pea under her bed. "You don't belong here!" she said, and she tossed it out the window. "Now I'll never see another pea again!"

But the pea grew into a plant, and the plant grew a pea.
And then another and another!
Penelopea frowned.
She wasn't expecting more peas to appear—ever!

"Not again! This time I'll make sure you disappear—all of you!" Penelopea popped a pea into her mouth.

And then another
and another!

And the more she ate,
the better they tasted.

"Pea-licious!"
said Penelopea.
"More peas, please!"

Penelopea's plant grew even more peas,
and she planted every single one.
Before long, Capital Pea
had plenty of peas,
and the king and queen
were positively pleased!

Now everyone in the kingdom
eats peas—and Penelopea
loves them most of all.

Parent and Caregiver Menu

~STARTERS~

Do you have a Princess Penelopea in your family? If so, you're not alone. As a parent, you want your child to enjoy a variety of healthy foods, but getting there isn't always easy. Maybe your child is afraid to try new foods, is selective about how foods are presented (e.g., not wanting the peas to touch the carrots), or prefers to stick to the same meal every night. Whatever the issue, consider whether or not any of these factors might explain your child's reluctance around some foods.

Biology

We are all programmed to prefer sweet over bitter flavors. In the past, this biological programming helped us avoid eating anything harmful. Today we have grocery stores full of safe foods, but our biology can *still* send us straight to the bakery instead of the vegetable aisle! Our biology can also contribute to food *neophobia*—a fear of new foods particularly common among children around two to six years of age. During this time, your child might also insist on eating one or two preferred foods and nothing else. This limited preference is called a *food jag*. Don't worry; with time most children want more variety.

Taste Buds

Children have many more taste buds than adults. Because of this, foods will taste more intense to children. So foods that taste sort of bitter to you may taste really bitter to your child!

Preferences

Some children are more sensitive than others to new tastes, textures, or smells. Children might also prefer certain flavors, textures, or colors. As adults, we have our favorites, too! As long as your child eats a variety of nutritious foods, likes and dislikes are okay and to be expected.

Medical Issues

Some health issues, like food allergies or digestive disorders, can contribute to picky eating. Some developmental issues, like autism spectrum disorder, can too.

Past Experiences

Sometimes children reject foods they associate with an unpleasant experience. For example, any food consumed before a bout of the stomach flu might not be a favorite—even years later!

Growth Spurts

Children can grow in spurts. When they are growing more quickly, they may be hungrier and more interested in food. When they are growing more slowly, they may be less interested in food and require less of it.

Independence

As children become more independent, they usually want to make more decisions on their own. Developing independence is important, but expect your child to say no to some things—including foods—as part of the process.

Seeing and Doing

Sometimes children who refuse to eat a variety of healthy foods live with adults who don't eat a variety of healthy foods. Sound familiar?

~THE MAIN COURSE~

If mealtime has turned into a battle, or you'd like to see your child eat a wider variety of healthy foods, consider these strategies. Keep in mind that you can control *what* food you serve and *how* and *when* you serve it. But *what to eat* and *how much to eat* are up to your child.

Start Early

Start offering a variety of healthy foods to your child at a young age. If you're unsure about what foods are appropriate for different ages, talk to your child's doctor.

Go Slowly

Introduce one new food at a time in a small portion. Be sure to pair it with a food your child already knows and likes. Be strategic. Introduce new foods when your child is hungry, and be matter of fact. No need to announce there is something new on the plate!

Keep Trying

In most cases, parents can help their children learn to like new foods by presenting those foods multiple times (between 5 and as many as 10 to 15 times). Be persistent! Keep offering new foods even if your child has refused them before.

Relax and Enjoy

Don't force your child to eat. Strategies like tricking, bribing, or punishing your child into eating don't tend to work and can backfire, leading to even bigger battles over food. Strive to provide healthy choices without pressure; meals are always better when everyone is relaxed!

Provide Choices

Give your child some control and choice when you can. For example, ask if your child would like an apple or banana, or raw versus cooked carrots. This strategy offers healthy options and gives your child some say, too.

Talk About "Everyday" and "Sometimes"

We all want what we can't have. When you restrict a certain food, your child may want it even more. Instead of teaching that foods are "good" or "bad," talk about "everyday" foods (like fruits and vegetables) and "sometimes" foods (like donuts and candy). Decide what "sometimes" means for your family, and try your best to stick to it.

Don't Make Dessert a Reward

It's okay for dessert to be a "sometimes" food enjoyed once in a while or in small portions. When dessert is an option, try not to make it a reward. Saying, "no dessert until you clean your plate" sends the message that dessert is the best part of the meal and the rest isn't as enjoyable.

Set an Example

Everyone in your family—and that means adults and children—can be a role model for healthy eating. When your family enjoys all sorts of healthy foods together, you set a great example for your child.

Watch What You Buy

Keep a variety of healthy snacks available and try to resist buying foods you don't want your child to eat. After all, it's hard to eat chips if there aren't any in the house! Watching what you buy also prevents you from having to say "no" when your child finds the chips in the cupboard.

Create Routines

Many picky eaters are "grazers" who snack on small amounts of food all day long. Try offering three meals and a limited number of snacks at the same time every day. That way, your child will know when to expect food and will probably feel hungry enough to eat it.

Turn Off and Tune In

Mealtime is family time. Toys, television, electronics, and other distractions are best reserved for before or after meals. After all, children generally eat better when they focus on eating. Sit down together as a family as often as you can.

Set a Time Limit

Set a time limit on meals and stick to it. Thirty minutes is usually long enough for children to finish a meal if they are hungry. When the time is up, end the meal and allow your child to be excused from the table. Asking children to sit longer probably *won't* result in more eating, but probably *will* make the meal unpleasant for everyone! If your child doesn't eat much at the table, try waiting until the next regular meal or snack time to present food instead of offering it right away.

Don't Be a Short-Order Cook

Make one meal for the family. If children know that refusing the meal you've made means you'll bring out a favorite, they may be less willing to try new foods. When your child refuses to eat at snacktime or mealtime, here are a couple of options. Offer food at the next scheduled time (even if it means waiting for breakfast the next morning). Don't worry—things usually balance out. Children who eat less at one meal generally eat more at the next. Another option? Offer *one* healthy choice you've agreed upon ahead of time—like veggie sticks and hummus or a fruit plate—if your child refuses what you've made. Whatever you decide, be consistent. Even if your child chooses not to eat, make staying at the table until the meal is finished a family habit for everyone!

Get Children Involved

Involve your children in mealtime. Let them choose a healthy option for dinner, or go with you to the grocery store to pick a healthy snack. Ask your children to help with food preparation—maybe washing fruit, pouring milk into oatmeal, or cracking eggs. Your meal might take a little longer to prepare, but most children are more interested in eating something they've helped to make.

Make Food Fun

Present foods in kid-friendly ways. Children like to dip, dunk, and swirl, so serve vegetables with healthy sauces. Taste tests, crunch tests, and smell tests are great ways to learn about food. Cut your child's sandwiches into anything—from triangles to dinosaurs! Make a meal menu and ask your child to take your order. Use silly names for food, like mini trees (broccoli) and penelopeas (green peas). Make Friday a finger-food night, or have an indoor picnic. Visit a farm to see where foods come from, or plant your own garden like Penelopea!

~THE FINAL COURSE~

Keep Perspective

In most cases, children who are choosy about food are getting the nutrition they need. If you're not sure, step back and consider the big picture by keeping track of what your child eats for one week. If your child seems to have energy and is growing, chances are your child is eating enough. But remember, even healthy children grow slowly at times.

Seek Help if You Need to

If you are concerned that your child's eating habits may be affecting his or her growth, development, or quality of life, speak with your child's doctor right away.

About the Authors

Susan D. Sweet, PhD, is a clinical child psychologist and mother of two. She has worked in hospital, school, and community-based settings and is passionate about children's mental health and well-being. Susan loves to cook (and eat!) and hopes to encourage children to view food as one of life's greatest adventures. This is her first book.

Brenda S. Miles, PhD, is a pediatric (pea-diatric!) neuropsychologist who has worked in hospital, rehabilitation, and school settings. While visiting her grandparents as a child, she tried lining up peas under her knife—proficiently and precisely—to avoid eating them. Her grandparents weren't fooled. Now Brenda thinks peas taste positively pleasing! She has written several books for children, including *Imagine a Rainbow: A Child's Guide for Soothing Pain,* and *Stickley Sticks to It! A Frog's Guide to Getting Things Done.* This is her first book about peas.

About the Illustrator

Valeria Docampo's inspiration for her art is rooted in everyday life: the eyes of a dog, the shape of a tree, the sound of rainfall, and the aromas of breakfast. Born in Buenos Aires, Argentina, she studied fine arts and graphic design at the University of Buenos Aires. She has illustrated several books for children, notably *Tout au Bord, La Vallée des Moulins, Phileas's Fortune,* and *Not Every Princess.*

About Magination Press

Magination Press is an imprint of the American Psychological Association, the largest scientific and professional organization representing psychologists in the United States and the largest association of psychologists worldwide.